14 Days

My name is Rosy Cole. I go to Read, which is a small private school on the Upper East Side of Manhattan. At Read our teacher, Mrs. Oliphant, assigns us books that are very interesting. Some are about adventure, some are about friendship, some are even about love, but none *of them* ever *is about romance.*

We have to find out about romance on our own. . . .

And so begins Project Romance. There is plenty of material on the subject in Barney's Book Nook; but why settle for *reading* about dates and proms when there are two teenagers right in Rosy's very own home? With a little hard work and ingenuity, Rosy will soon have her sisters living out the romances of her dreams — or so she thinks!

This is a Junior Library Guild selection, chosen as an outstanding book for boys and girls (A Group).

Books by Sheila Greenwald

ALL THE WAY TO WITS' END
IT ALL BEGAN WITH JANE EYRE: OR, THE
  SECRET LIFE OF FRANNY DILLMAN
GIVE US A GREAT BIG SMILE, ROSY COLE
BLISSFUL JOY AND THE SATs: A MULTIPLE-
  CHOICE ROMANCE
WILL THE REAL GERTRUDE HOLLINGS PLEASE
  STAND UP?
VALENTINE ROSY
ROSY COLE'S GREAT AMERICAN GUILT CLUB
ALVIN WEBSTER'S SUREFIRE PLAN FOR SUCCESS
  (AND HOW IT FAILED)
WRITE ON, ROSY! (A YOUNG AUTHOR IN CRISIS)
ROSY'S ROMANCE

ROSY's Romance

by Sheila Greenwald

Joy Street Books
Little, Brown and Company
BOSTON   TORONTO   LONDON

First edition

Library of Congress Cataloging-in-Publication Data

Greenwald, Sheila.
  Rosy's romance/by Sheila Greenwald.
     p. cm.
  Summary: Rosy and her friend Hermione attempt to help Rosy's teenage sisters live out the romantic fantasies they have been reading about in paperback.

  ISBN 0-316-32704-2
  [1. Sisters — Fiction.] I. Title.

PZ7.G852Rr1989
[Fic] — dc19
                                                        88-32270
                                                             CIP
                                                              AC

Joy Street Books are published by Little, Brown and Company (Inc.)

BP

10 9 8 7 6 5 4 3 2 1

Published simultaneously in Canada
by Little, Brown & Company (Canada) Limited

PRINTED IN THE UNITED STATES OF AMERICA

For Ben

ROSY's Romance

Chapter One

My name is Rosy Cole. I go to Read, which is a small private school on the Upper East Side of Manhattan. At Read our teacher, Mrs. Oliphant, assigns us books that are very interesting. Some are about adventure, some are about friendship, some are even about love, but *none* of them *ever* is about romance.

We have to find out about romance on our own.

This is no problem, thanks to Barney's Book Nook, around the corner from my school.

I can read a whole book in only three sessions after school,

with hardly anyone noticing.

My friend Hermione Wong, who is in my class and lives in my building, has practically the entire collection of Sugerwater High and numbers one through twelve of Sakrinhill Quints.

Since I have only one of each, Hermione is always complaining. "I've read both your books, Rosy," she says. "It isn't fair when you keep borrowing mine."

What isn't fair is that my mother won't let me buy more of the books I love. She calls them "trash." When I try to point out some of the things she reads, she gets sulky and says she's old enough to know her books have nothing to do with real life.

I have to sneak my books into the house

and disguise them once they get there.

Three months ago when I first saw Debbie and Hermione reading Sakrinhill Quints, I said, "What is that goop?"

"It's not goop," Debbie said. "It's all about dates and boyfriends and being a teen. You should try one."

So I did.

She was right.

Even though I was reading a book, it was more like watching a movie or a TV show where something happens in front of your eyes.

It made me think of Lucas Ashe, my friend Wendy's brother, who goes to Finchely. It was Lucas who got the boys to come to my Valentine party and who sent me the Valentine that made me feel happy and nervous at the same time. I never thought I'd find out about feeling this way until I got older, but suddenly I was finding out about it right now, in a book.

One afternoon at the Book Nook, Hermione selected Sakrinhill numbers thirteen, fourteen, and fifteen.

"You can't read them all at once," I pointed out while the sales clerk rang them up.

"It's so unfair the way you keep borrowing my books," Hermione grumbled as she opened the bag and handed me number fifteen. "I've read your three and six twice."

Neither of us could wait to get home and settle down to what Debbie calls "a good read."

Number fifteen was so gripping I never noticed that it had gotten dark out. By the time I had to set the table, I was only one chapter from the end.

When we sat down to dinner, my mother said, "Rosy, is there something happening on the floor that the rest of us should know about?"

My sister Pippa grabbed the book off my lap and held it up for everyone to see. "*Prom Time*," she read off the cover.

"That junk again." My mother frowned.

"It's not junk." I could hear the wobble in my voice so I didn't say more.

"Tell us about it," my father said gently.

"It's all about being a teen," I said.

My sister Anitra burst out laughing. "Pippa and I could tell you about that."

I looked at them and suddenly realized something amazing. Pippa and Anitra were *teens*.

Hermione might have the books, one through fifteen, but I had the *real thing* right under my nose!

As soon as dinner was over, I called Hermione to tell her my discovery.

"Pippa and Anitra!" she hooted.

"They're teens," I insisted. "They just don't know how to do it."

"Who's going to tell them?"

I didn't have to answer because Hermione said, "I'll be at your place tomorrow after school. This is clearly a VITD" — our code for Very Important Thing to Discuss.

Chapter Two

The first thing Hermione and I did when we came home from school the next day was check out Anitra and Pippa. They were in Anitra's room listening to a new album with their friends Jojo and Pete.

"They may be teens and those may be boys," Hermione commented, "but the Sakrinhill Quints wouldn't let them through the door."

"Come with me." I took Hermione into the living room, where we kept our family photo album. "I want to show you some interesting pictures."

ANITRA AGE 10

ANITRA AGE . 14

PIPPA AGE 10

PIPPA AGE 13

"Why are these interesting?" she asked.

"It means that they can change. They did it before. They'll do it again."

Hermione stared at the photos. "But, Rosy, they need a complete overhaul. Hair to shoes."

"And that's just the beginning," I said. "The end will be dates and crushes and parties and . . ." I was trying to think of the most exciting thing.

"A prom." Hermione sighed.

"Of course!"

A prom would be the most exciting thing of all.

"What will we call this?" Hermione loves to find official titles for our projects.

I closed my eyes and I could just see what the next photo in our family album would look like.

"Project Romance," I said.

"Beautiful." Hermione closed her eyes too. "Dreamy."

Because of Project Romance, things began to happen. One: I got no more arguments from Hermione about borrowing her books. Two: We began to collect supplies for Project Romance. My room started to fill up.

Since Friday is a half day at the Read School, Hermione and I decided to go crosstown right after lunch and check out my sisters' school, Foxley Prep.

Just before the final bell, our teacher, Mrs. Oliphant, announced that our spring dance with Finchely would take place in four weeks, and we should all mark down the date because we wouldn't want to miss it.

"I wouldn't mind missing it," Hermione groaned. "Remember how last time Charlie Hicks and Micky Buttonwiser painted their hands with indelible ink and got it all over my new sweater?"

"Yuck." Debbie rolled her eyes. "And they started a chalk fight."

"That was months ago," Mary pointed out. "I think we've all matured since then."

"I agree." Wendy nodded. "They were very good at Rosy's Valentine party.

Lucas said he had a wonderful time."

He did? Hearing that Lucas had a wonderful time at my party made me feel happy and giddy and surprised all at once.

On the way to Foxley Prep, Hermione kept asking me if Foxley was anything like Sugerwater High.

"It's hard to say," I said, trying to put her off.

Most of the students at Sugerwater High are beautiful and handsome and rich. They live in big houses and have plenty of spending money. Some of them are cheerleaders. Some of them are athletes. Some of them want to go to Hollywood. Some of them are from "the wrong side of the tracks" and don't have much money, but even so they enjoy themselves falling in love and going to beach parties and drive-ins and dances and picnics and shopping for wonderful clothes. I wasn't sure Foxley students would measure up.

When we walked into the building, I knew I was right to be worried. Foxley Prep teens were nothing like the teens at Sugerwater High.

But then I saw the bulletin board, and my worries vanished.

We checked our calendars to see how much time we had.

Hermione moaned. "Oh, no! It's the same night as our dance with Finchely."

"No problem," I said, and we both laughed because we knew we'd be willing to forget about Finchely in a minute if we had to.

All the way home we talked about my sisters' prom. We couldn't help checking out some of the shops on Madison Avenue for clothes ideas.

"I can just imagine Anitra in something like that." Hermione pointed. "Remember how Suki 'swirls in front of her mirror in the silver ruffled gown.'"

" 'Awaiting fabulously handsome Ron
Ronson, who would ring the doorbell and
whisk her off to the Junior Prom,' " I went
on. " 'Encircling her tiny waist with his

23

strong basketball player's arms,' " I finished quoting from *Prom Time*, and, sure enough, a warm feeling went right through me, the way it did every time I read that part.

When we got back to my apartment, we went to check on Anitra and Pippa. They had just come home and were in Anitra's room listening to a new album.

"What's up?" Anitra hollered.

"Are you going out tonight?" I asked.

"Jojo and Pete are coming by. It's Friday. Why?"

"Can we help you prepare for your dates?" Hermione asked.

"Dates?" They both looked blank. "Isn't that something you stuff with an almond and roll in coconut flakes?" Anitra joked.

"Dates are boyfriends," Hermione explained carefully. "When you're a teen, you get happy and excited about seeing them. You do your hair and your nails. Then you put on some very terrific clothes and you spray very wonderful perfume all over yourself."

"Hair?" Pippa pulled on the Mohawk she was beginning to let grow out. "Sorry, I don't seem to have any."

"Nails?" Anitra held out her hand. "I don't seem to have any of those either." I looked. She didn't.

"We can fix that," Hermione said excitedly. I thought she was joking, but then I remembered our Project Romance supplies in my room. Two full boxes of Penny's Press-On nails, and Mrs. Wong's old wigs.

Only minutes later we were back in Anitra's room, ready to begin.

"What's going on here?" Anitra giggled. "Are we playing beauty parlor?"

I was showing her how easy Penny's Press-Ons were to apply.

"Holy smoke." Pippa gazed at her reflection. Hermione had just put Mrs. Wong's Cleopatra wig on her head. "Jojo and Pete will pass out when they see us."

"What do we wear to go with our nails and hair?" Anitra wondered.

"I know." I ran off to find the dresses my mother had bought my sisters for my cousin Jason's wedding three years ago.

"You've got to be kidding, Rosy," Pippa said, holding the dress under her chin and twirling around. I sprayed her with Mom's Made for Love cologne. Anitra began to sing "I feel pretty, oh so pretty," when the doorbell rang.

"The dates are here," I told Hermione. We ran to let them in. It was too good to be true. Everything was happening just the way we planned it.

It *was* too good to be true.

Just when we thought we were making progress.

"Say, what's up?" Jojo blinked. "Halloween?"

"Sort of." Pippa yanked off the wig and did her vampire hiss. She couldn't get her nails off fast enough.

Anitra threw her dress on the bed and her nails on top of them.

"So, let's go," Pete said.

"What are you going to do, dressed like that?" Hermione asked. She was blinking as if she couldn't believe her eyes.

"We're going to do what we always do," Pete told her. "Hang out."

Hermione and I looked at each other. "This is romance?" she asked me.

"Oh, yes," I assured her, even though I wasn't so sure myself. "And better than Sugerwater High because it's real life."

"It's real life, all right," Hermione agreed. "But I'm not so sure it's better."

"That's our job," I reminded her. "Project Romance."

Chapter Three

Hermione called her parents to ask if she could stay at my house for dinner and sleep over. We had to work on our strategy. We had three hours before Anitra and Pippa would be back with Jojo and Pete.

After dessert my parents went to the movies. We were alone in the apartment. We decided to perfect our spying techniques.

"We can watch the front door and the hallway without being seen if we stand behind my bedroom door and leave it open just a crack." I showed Hermione. "Then we can track Anitra and Pippa and their dates right into the living room or the kitchen, just by creeping into the dining room. From the dining room, we get a clear view in either direction."

"We have to be very quiet," she said.

"We have to slither," I said.

We got into our pajamas and practiced.

By eleven o'clock when the door clicked open, we were so good at slithering that the couple who came in never knew we tailed them from the hall to the kitchen to the door of the living room.

"Oh, boy," Hermione whispered. "This is it."

"I told you we'd find romance," I reminded her.

"It's like number fourteen." Hermione sighed. We both knew the title of number fourteen was *Perfect Love*.

We were too excited to talk after that because they began to kiss. They kissed and kissed.

Then I heard a voice say, "It's time for bed, honey," and the light went on. It was only Mom and Dad.

Hermione and I looked at each other. We didn't bother to slither, we just tip-toed back to my room.

"I'm exhausted." Hermione yawned. "I can't go through this again."

Neither could I. " 'It's time for bed, honey,' " I quoted my mother.

"Your parents have the only romance in this family," Hermione accused me.

I got into bed and pulled the covers over my ears. "Not after our project gets going." I tried to sound hopeful, but I was beginning to think we would need a miracle to turn my sisters into even Kim, the most unpopular Quint.

"We don't need a miracle." Hermione read my mind in the dark. "We need to find them new boyfriends."

That sounded like a big order to me, but I was too sleepy to argue about it.

Since the next day was Saturday, Hermione and I had time to begin to work and plan.

My father sent us out to buy him a newspaper. He gave us a little extra for ice creams, but at the newsstand we knew exactly what to use the "little extra" for. We found the perfect research material for our project.

We even considered spending the afternoon at home to go over the information, but the matinee at the Triplex was too good to miss. Before Project Romance, it would have been hard to choose between *Honk the Horrible* and *Fun High,* but now we needed *Fun High* for our work.

In the lobby we bumped into Charlie
Hicks and Lucas Ashe.

"I thought you'd be here, Rosy," Lucas
said. "I told Charlie you wouldn't miss
Honk the Horrible."

"We're here to see *Fun High*, with
Patsy Dingwall," I said.

"You're always busy," Lucas com-
plained. "I haven't seen you since Valentine's Day."

"I see you and Charlie playing catch in front of my school almost every other day," I reminded him.

"I didn't know you saw me." He got red in the face.

"Anyway, I want to thank you for getting the boys to come to my party. It would have been a huge flop if it hadn't been for you."

"Anytime you need me, just whistle." I could tell Lucas liked this line because it gave him the chance to go ahead and do it.

"Who knows?" I shrugged. "Project Romance might need a consultant down the line."

"Project Romance?" Lucas looked mystified.

"I can't talk about it now," I said. "It's still classified."

"That's one thing I like about you, Rosy. You make everything," he said, looking around him, "like a spy movie."

"Thanks." I helped myself to a handful of his popcorn and wondered what the other things were that he liked about me. I decided not to ask him. He might say he was just kidding and laugh about it, and I'd feel awful.

Still, I was wondering so much I almost forgot to pay attention to Patsy Dingwall in *Fun High*. Poor Patsy lived on the wrong side of the tracks, but she got asked to the Senior Prom by handsome and rich football star Rob Bancroft. All the snooty rich girls ganged up on Patsy. All the snooty poor girls ganged up on Patsy. Everybody was jealous of Patsy. Finally Patsy tells Rob she can't go to the prom, which causes him to forget to see a traffic light and nearly get killed by a truck, which makes everybody sorry and love Rob and Patsy, who go to the prom in the end.

The characters in the movie reminded me of the characters in Sakrinhill and Sugerwater. You could tell how thrilled they all were to be teens.

"It's just like I said, they need new boy-friends," Hermione said when we left the theater. "If Jojo and Pete were like Rob

Bancroft, Anitra and Pippa would see to it they were as cute as Patsy."

"That's it," I agreed. "That's been the problem all along. They have the wrong boyfriends."

All the way home we had our eyes out for the right boyfriends, but finding them

turned out to be harder than we thought.

"I guess we have to work with what we've got," Hermione said.

"What we've got are Anitra and Pippa and Jojo and Pete," I sighed. Back at my place, we went to check out my sisters.

It wasn't going to be easy.

"Aren't you going out tonight?" I asked them. "It's Saturday."

"The Saturday before exam week." Anitra didn't look up from her book.

"But you need a break."

"Why this sudden interest in our social life?" Pippa asked.

"You're teens," I reminded her. "Terrific, exciting things are happening in your world."

"Yup." She nodded. "Final exams and term papers."

"Boyfriends, dates, proms," Hermione suggested.

"Who needs boyfriends, dates, and proms?" Pippa exchanged a look with Anitra that really upset me.

"You do," I said, "only you just don't know how to do it. You wear these terrible clothes and play that stupid music and go out with those grubby-looking guys."

"Poor Rosy." Anitra closed her book and made a sad face at me. "I guess you'd like a couple of new sisters."

All of a sudden I felt rotten. "It's just that I wish you'd try."

"Try what?" Anitra actually seemed serious.

"A real date," I said. "A dinner date."

Anitra and Pippa began to shake their heads.

"Just invite Jojo and Pete to dinner Friday night," I pleaded. "We'll do the rest."

"Here?" Pippa pointed to the dining room. "What will Mom and Dad say?"

"Don't worry about it. I'll take care of them." I knew my parents had plans of their own for Friday. Mom had written it down on the kitchen calendar.

"Okay with me." Pippa shrugged.

"You're on, Rosy." Anitra began to giggle. Soon we were all laughing. They were laughing because they thought it was such a weird idea. But now Hermione and I had the chance we'd been waiting for.

Later when I told my mother the plan, she said, "Dinner for four people is a real responsibility. Are you sure you can handle it?"

"We've got five whole days to prepare," I pointed out.

"All right," my mother agreed. "When you've decided on your menu, let me know so I can give you the shopping money. I'm sure you aren't thinking of caviar and filet mignon."

As a matter of fact, *Menus for Romance* had suggested those very items at the top of the list.

Monday in lunch period, Hermione and I rushed through our peanut butter sandwiches so we could work out our dinner menu.

"Let's start with True Love Salad," Hermione said, "and follow it with Chicken for Flirting."

True Love Salad included the petals of two pink roses and rose water in the dressing. Chicken for Flirting had fifteen steps.

"True Love Salad?" Debbie said, as she choked on her milk. "What's that for?"

"Project Romance," Hermione said, as if it were common knowledge. In about two more minutes, it was. Everybody in my class wanted to know about it.

"Can I come over and help?" Mary Settleheim asked. "My upside-down pineapple cake is a sure thing. They'll fall in love with it."

"The point is not to fall in love with the cake, but with each other."

"Like in Sakrinhill or Sugerwater," I explained.

"A real live Sakrinhill," Debbie crooned. "How amazing. How fantastic."

"A whole dinner party?" Christi McCurry seemed impressed. "That's a lot to handle."

"Not if you're organized," I said.

"And we're very well organized," Hermione added.

We couldn't understand why everybody kept telling us a dinner party was a lot of work. All we had to do was follow the directions in our cookbook.

Friday afternoon after school we did just that.

1. MAKE a list of what we need (ask Mom for $)
2. Shop
3. Prepare food for cooking

4. Cook

5. Set The Table

6. Check Dinner

7. Prepare food for presentation.

Actually, after a while, I began to see that a dinner party involved more than I thought.

8. Put on a smile and welcome your guests.

But finally our romantic dinner was ready. It had candles (glued into holders), flowers (taped to the vase), Chicken for Flirting (burnt but disguised by True Love Salad).

It had Anitra and Pippa and Jojo and
Pete

and lots of dishes.

"They aren't Sakrinhill," Hermione
said, peeking at the two couples from behind the kitchen door.

"Don't worry," I said. "This is just the
beginning. The prom will be different."

Chapter Four

But five whole days went by, and not a soul in my family even mentioned the prom. Then Thursday night at dinner my mother said, "I got a notice from your school, Rosy. The dance with Finchely is in two weeks. Would you like a new dress?"

"A new dress? To get ink smeared on it by Micky Buttonwiser? And chalk dust from Charlie Hicks? You've got to be kidding!"

"But they behaved very nicely at your Valentine party."

"That was such a super party," Anitra gushed.

"It had everything," Pippa said. "Pin the tail on the donkey, and musical chairs, and punch, and little heart-shaped cakes, and singing."

"It was a good party," I interrupted, "but it wasn't a prom."

"A prom," Pippa hooted, "is a ridiculous waste of time and money."

"I couldn't agree more." Anitra nodded.

After dinner I called Hermione and told her the bad news.

"All that means is, they haven't been asked," Hermione said.

When I hung up the phone, I told my mother Hermione was coming over. "We have a very tough assignment," I explained.

I wasn't lying.

This wasn't homework, but it was going to be practically impossible.

"They don't sound right," I said.

"How should they sound?" Hermione asked.

"Like a boy wrote them."

Hermione looked grim. "How do we do that?"

"We need an inspiration," I said. "Maybe we'll get one tomorrow."

The very next day it happened. We were just leaving school at three-thirty, when who should we see playing catch on the corner? Lucas and Charlie. Lucas

waved, and instead of just waving back and walking away, I ran up to him and gave a loud whistle. He knew exactly what I meant.

"What's up?" Charlie asked.

"I don't know," Hermione said. But Lucas put the ball in his pocket and followed me across the street to Central Park. Hermione and Charlie ran after us.

"We need a consultation for Project Romance," I explained. They sat down on a bench. I gave Lucas and Charlie each a piece of paper and a pencil. "In your own words, write a note inviting a girl to a prom."

"It's not a prom." Lucas looked terrified. "It's just a dumb dance with Read."

"My *sisters'* prom," I said. "We need to help get them there."

"You want me and Charlie to take them?"

"We want you and Charlie to ask them

for their boyfriends. Jojo and Pete are very shy."

"Do these shy guys know what we're going to do?"

I shook my head. "Not yet."

"I'm not so sure about this." Lucas looked down at the bench. "I think there may be a law against it. Mail fraud."

"Don't worry," I assured him. "It will be fine."

They began to write. I was glad to see how seriously they took my project. When they finished, they looked exhausted.

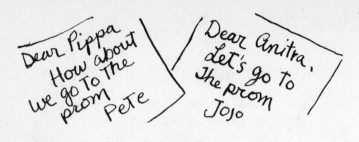

"That's it?" I asked.

"What else?" Charlie seemed surprised.

"Something romantic," Hermione said.

"Oh, I get it." Charlie fell down on one
knee in front of Hermione and grabbed
her hand. "My white steed awaits us

under yonder tree. Let us be off to the castle."

"How about it, Rosy?" Lucas signaled to where Charlie's horse was supposed to be waiting.

"Four on a horse?" I gasped. "Is it safe?"

We all pretended to get on a horse and ride into the old playground where we used to go before there was school.

Back then we sat in the sandbox and made castles with moats around them and mountains with tunnels through them. Sometimes we went down the slide, which seemed a mile high, or swung on the swings so that our stomachs felt left behind. We called that the "heebie jeebies." (It was something like getting a Valentine card from Lucas, only different because that was before we knew anything about romance. That was when we were just friends having fun.)

We didn't stay long because we had serious work to do. "Thanks for your help," I told Lucas and Charlie. "If there's anything we can do for you, let us know."

"I'd like to see what's so great about

these guys that you think your sisters want them to be dates," Lucas said.

"Come to my place at seven o'clock on the twenty-sixth of May," I said. "If these invitations work, they'll be there and headed for the prom."

As soon as we waved good-bye to Lucas and Charlie, Hermione said, "The letters are a good idea, but will Jojo and Pete want to go with Pippa and Anitra, or will it be like *One-way Romance?*"

One-way Romance was the title of book number six. Suki, the most beautiful Quint, falls in love with tennis star Tip Topper, only to find that he doesn't love her back.

"You're right," I said. "We have to send invites from Anitra and Pippa to Jojo and Pete so it won't seem one way."

"And we can write those ourselves." Hermione laughed. "We know how to sound like girls."

As it turned out, it wasn't easy to sound like a girl inviting a guy to a prom. We worked on the letters for almost an hour, and then we remembered to look at number ten, *P.S. I've Got a Crush on You*. In the book, one of the Quints writes anonymous love letters to Tod Jameson, the dreamy newcomer in town. Sure enough, we found exactly the right letter to use.

Dearest,
How I dream
of your arms around
me on that magic
night of nights when
the music is soft
and the air is sweet
and everything is dreamy
because I'm dancing
with you...

We folded up all the letters and tried to figure out what kind of envelopes to put them into. Then we figured out how to mail them. The only thing we never figured out was that three days later when they arrived, Jojo and Pete would be there watching while Anitra and Pippa opened them.

"What's this?" Anitra ripped open her invitation while Pippa did the same.

"An invitation to the prom." She gasped and turned to Jojo. "From *you*."

"I got one, too." Pippa waved her invitation around her head.

"From who?" Pete said angrily.

"From you, you cool dude." Pippa tapped him with the envelope.

Pete blushed and snatched the invitation from her hand. "You don't want to go, though. It's a joke."

"Maybe I *do* want to go." Pippa winked at Anitra. "If it's a joke, it's a good one."

"Somebody sent us invites from you and Anitra, but we knew it was a joke. What kind of sap would want to go to a prom?"

"Sap?" Pippa turned the shade of orange red she does when she is very angry. "Maybe the kind of sap who thought it might be fun to go with you."

"Don't get mad," Pete said, too late. "It just never dawned on me that you'd send us invites."

It never dawned on me that sending

those invitations would cause my sisters and their boyfriends to fight. This was nothing like *P.S. I've Got a Crush on You.*

"We never sent you invitations," Anitra told Pete. "Somebody is playing a trick."

"Somebody who?" Jojo said as if he didn't believe her.

"Do you honestly think that Pippa and I would play a trick like that?" It was Anitra's turn to get furious.

"Well, why is it such a horrible idea to go with *us?*" Pete hollered. "What are we? Slobs?"

Hermione and I looked at each other. Was he a mind reader?

"I wouldn't go to a prom with you if you asked me on bended knees," Pippa snarled.

"Don't worry," Pete said, "you won't get the chance."

"You took the words right out of my mouth," Jojo told him, and they left.

"Good riddance," Pippa called after them.

Hermione and I went to my room and closed the door.

"Project Romance is dead," she said grimly.

I flopped on my bed and looked at the floor. Number seven, *Say It with Roses,* looked back at me from under my slipper. I held it up and showed it to Hermione.

"It's like a sign," she gasped.

In number seven, Susan, the glamorous Quint, has an argument with her boyfriend, Hank. Even though they are crazy about each other, the misunderstanding is driving them apart. They each get the idea of sending the other a single red rose.

Because of the gift of the rose they make up and begin to date again.

Hermione calculated. "Four roses at two dollars apiece will set us back an allowance and a half each."

"I saw some marked down to a dollar at the vegetable store," I recalled. "We can pick them up on the way home from school."

"It can't be soon enough," Hermione said, looking worried. "The prom is only eight days away."

The notes we attached to the roses were easy.

"I don't believe how gooey Jojo's gotten." Anitra wrinkled her nose when she read her note. "I mean, roses and proms."

Pippa waved her rose over her head like a flag. "Pretending they didn't send us invitations and then pretending we sent invitations to them."

"What if they're pretending now?" Anitra asked.

"Let's play along." Pippa giggled. "Let's say we'd love to go to the prom with them."

"But then we'll have to go," Anitra warned.

"Okay, so we'll go, the same way they asked us."

"You mean like a joke."

"Like a joke." Pippa began to laugh and Anitra joined in. The telephone rang. It was Pete. Pippa rolled her eyes and listened to him. "I sent *you* a rose?" She covered her mouth to keep from laughing

into the receiver. "That was very sweet of me. This is so romantic, how could I say no to the prom? How could you say no to the prom? I guess if we can't say no, what we're saying is yes."

When she hung up, Anitra called Jojo.

They spoke in whispers, and when the conversation was over she told Pippa it was set. "Now all we need are dresses."

"Dresses?" I said from behind the door. "We could window-shop and report back to you what we find."

"You could." Anitra laughed. "But I don't think what you find is what we'll want to wear."

Hermione and I decided not to get our hopes up. Still, we had hopes.

Chapter Five

The next day was Saturday. We set out to shop at eleven. On the corner were Lucas and Charlie looking at the tree on our corner with binoculars.

"What are you doing?" I asked Lucas.

"Bird-watching," he said. "This is a good corner. Last week somebody spotted a blue jay here. Where are you going, Rosy?"

"To find prom dresses for my sisters," I said.

"If we came along we could give you the boy's point of view," he said.

We told them they could come with us,

though I was afraid they might tease us about shopping.

On Lexington Avenue, Lucas pointed to the window of the Lomax Thrift Shop.

PROM CLOTHES 1956

"Aren't we lucky that styles have changed since then," Hermione said.

"How could anybody go out on the street like that," I said.

When we stopped laughing, we checked out Krazy Klose and Pretty Things, and then we went in to have a soda and review what we had seen.

"The blue chiffon for Anitra," I said.

"And the silver for Pippa," Hermione added.

"You'd look good in that too, Rosy." Lucas gave me a funny sideways smile. He looked like he was about to make another joke, so I blew my straw paper at him and crossed my eyes.

But when we got home, my sisters were opening shopping bags to show my mother what they had already bought.

"Where did you get those?" Mom groaned.

"The Lomax Thrift Shop!" Pippa shouted.

Anitra pulled her dress over her blue jeans. "They're just like the roses and the prom invitations. Corny."

Mom shook her head. "There's a cigarette hole in the skirt." She sighed. "And the material smells of mold."

"Eau de Mildew." Pippa danced by on tiptoe. "Our new perfume." She twirled in front of the mirror. "Jojo and Pete will get the joke, Mom. It will serve them right for sending those silly roses and those mushy notes."

"This isn't working," Hermione grumbled under her breath. "They don't understand romance at all."

That Monday, everybody in my class began to talk about the dance with Finchely.

"I'm wearing my new cotton knit from Beegee's," Effie Winship said.

"I don't know what to wear," Mary Settleheim groaned. "I guess I have to go shopping with my mother. She thinks the dance is such a cute idea."

"What are you going to wear, Rosy?" Effie asked me.

"I don't know," I said. In fact, I didn't want to think about the Finchely dance, because whenever I did, I imagined how I would feel sitting by myself on a folding chair while everybody danced around me. I once read about a girl who had that happen. She spent two hours on a folding chair pretending she was having fun watching her classmates enjoy themselves, when all the time she was miserable and couldn't wait for it to be over.

In the afternoon when my mother came home from work, she was carrying a large box. "I got you something to wear to your dance." She opened the box as if what was inside would make me the happiest girl in the world.

"Well?" she asked. "What do you think?"

"It's like something from a book," I said, and I didn't mean *Prom Time*.

Hermione called to tell me that she and her mother had just come back from shopping for a dress. She came over to show it to me.

"There wasn't much choice," Hermione
grumbled. "In the preteen department,
everything is preteen."

I knew what she meant. She meant that nothing looked like Sakrinhill or Sugerwater. It wasn't fair. We had to sit around in dumb clothes at the dumb Finchely dance, worrying about whether or not somebody would ask one of us to be his partner, while teens got "whisked off" to proms in glamorous gowns.

"Let's think of something to do that will cheer us up," Hermione said.

We went into my sisters' closets and took out the prom dresses. It wouldn't hurt to try them on.

Even though they were sort of old and moldy, they worked like magic.

Right in the middle, Anitra and Pippa walked in. "Say, that's terrific." Pippa clapped her hands.

We got our Press-On nails and Mrs. Wong's wigs, and in only a few minutes we were all made over.

Pippa and Anitra liked the nails and

wigs so much, they decided to use them for the prom.

We really were cheered up.

Chapter Six

The next day in the lunchroom we told everybody in our class about how we got Anitra and Pippa to go to a prom. "We did it through Project Romance," Hermione boasted. Then I explained about the invitations and the roses.

"That is so thrilling," Natalie cried. "Just like Sakrinhill Quints or Sugerwater High. I wonder, would you consider using my little gold heart-shaped locket and my silver bangle in their wardrobe?"

"My mother has a makeup kit with ten colors of eye shadow," Mary said. "She lets me borrow it. I could bring it over."

"What about an evening bag?" Jenny

asked. "My mother has a collection. I know she could spare a couple."

By the time lunch was over we had so many offers we had to write them down.

It seemed everybody in my class was more interested in Anitra and Pippa going to the prom at Foxley than going to the Finchely dance.

Every afternoon for the rest of the week, somebody in my class either brought a package to school or dropped it off at my building.

Jenny brought two beaded evening bags, Christi found a pair of silver shoes. Natalie left off the gold locket and the silver bangle.

On Thursday Pippa came into my room and looked around. "Rosy, why are you collecting evening bags and silver shoes?"

"They're things for you to wear to your prom," I said.

"Accessories." Pippa slipped her foot into Christi's shoe. It fit. "How did you know?" She picked up one of the evening bags.

Anitra opened the door and handed me a letter that had come in the mail.

"Rosy's been out collecting junk for us to wear to the prom," Pippa told her. They each scooped up a handful of things and went to try them on.

I opened my letter.

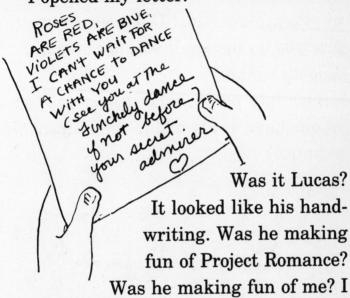

ROSES
ARE RED,
VIOLETS ARE BLUE,
I CAN'T WAIT FOR
A CHANCE TO DANCE
WITH YOU
(see you at The
Finchely dance
if not before)
your secret
admirer
♡

Was it Lucas? It looked like his handwriting. Was he making fun of Project Romance? Was he making fun of me? I folded the letter up and put it in my jewelry box and tried to forget about it.

Friday is a half day at Read. Just before we were dismissed, Mrs. Oliphant had a reminder. "Be at the Finchely gym by seven," she said. "Tell your parents to pick you up by ten. It will be three hours of loads of fun."

The only person who looked as if she would have loads of fun was Mrs. Oliphant.

When we went to Vinny's Pizza for lunch, everybody wanted to sit next to me or Hermione. It was as if we were Princess Di and Fergie.

"I would give anything to see them get ready to go to the prom," Linda said.

"Me, too." Debbie nodded.

"We've got our own dance to go to," I reminded them.

"But maybe we could just look at Anitra and Pippa's dresses?" Mary pleaded. "Like a fashion show."

"Oh, please say yes." Linda grabbed my arm and squeezed.

"It might be better if you just tried to imagine them," I said.

"It would definitely be better if you tried to imagine them," Hermione agreed. But everybody kept begging us, and finally we gave in.

When we opened the closet and held up the dresses, nobody said anything for a minute, and then Mary murmured, "They seem sort of grubby."

I was glad she hadn't gotten a look at Jojo and Pete.

"Seeing them on Anitra and Pippa makes all the difference," I told her.

Saturday morning, Hermione came over early. Anitra and Pippa were still asleep. We fixed breakfast for them, but they didn't get up.

Finally we couldn't wait any longer.

"What's that?" Anitra woke up suddenly, pointing to the breakfast tray we had just brought in.

"Today's the special day," I reminded her. "We wanted to set the right mood."

"For what?"

We knew she must be joking.

"Oh, the prom," she remembered.

We left her breakfast on the bed and headed for Pippa's room.

"Oh, no, not now." Pippa seemed to be having a nightmare. We put her tray on the floor and waited half an hour before we checked again. She'd eaten everything but the rose.

"Can we do anything to help?" we asked my sisters.

"What did you have in mind, Rosy?" Pippa said.

"Stockings," I said. "You forgot about stockings."

"Stockings?" She looked baffled. "You mean, to wear with our shoes?"

Actually, it was to wear with Christi's shoes. Christi had told me she didn't want anybody's bare feet in her new pumps.

"Sure," Anitra answered for both of them. "Buy us some knee-hi's."

They gave us money and we went to Mandy's Hot Socks where we bought two pairs of one-size-fits-all Made-for-Romance silver mesh paisley lace stockings.

When we got to our building, we saw Lucas and Charlie dribbling a basketball on the sidewalk. "What's in the bag?" Lucas called after me.

"It's secret," I said. I didn't want to talk to him after his anonymous note. I didn't want to be teased.

"Why do you think Lucas and Charlie are always hanging around our building and our school?" Hermione asked me in the lobby.

"How should I know?" I said. Then I thought of something. "Maybe Charlie has a crush on you."

Hermione turned as red as a tomato. "It's you, Rosy," she said. "Lucas has a crush on you."

"I call that stupid," I said.

"I call it Rosy's Romance," Hermione said, grinning at me as if I were one of the Sakrinhill Quints.

Chapter Seven

As soon as we got home, Mary called. "Are they nervous?"

"No." Actually it was Hermione and I who were nervous. To calm down, we re-read parts of *Prom Time* out loud.

Kim saw her reflection in the hall mirror. Who was that gorgeous slender girl
with the honey blond mane of curls and
the swirls of pink organza falling like a
cloud from tanned silky shoulders? She
could hardly believe it was herself. Shy,
bookworm Kim. In a minute handsome
Nick Nichols had wrapped his dark tux-
edoed arms around her slim waist. A
thrill went through her. This was it.
Prom night. The dream night of her life
was really coming true.

At five Jenny called. "Are they getting
ready now?"

"Not yet."

At six Pippa put on Mrs. Wong's "Marilyn" wig and eyelashes. Anitra pulled up her knee-hi's and stuck nails on the fingers of her left hand. They both stepped into their dresses. Anitra opened Mary's mother's makeup kit. Pippa chose a dark purple lipstick. "This is the one," she said, and smeared it over her lips.

Anitra did the same. They both powdered their faces and rubbed rouge on their cheeks.

I looked at the clock and suddenly realized it was time to get ready for the Finchely dance. I saw myself on my wallflower chair in my wallflower dress, watching everybody else dancing around, and my stomach went down like an express elevator.

"I suppose we better get dressed," Hermione whispered. I could tell her stomach was on the same elevator.

By six-forty-five, we were dressed. My

parents came into the foyer to have a look at us.

"How very sweet," my mother said.

Sweet?

If I had had any hope for the Finchely dance, that ended it. Sweet girls ate lots of potato chips and went home early.

Just then Anitra and Pippa swept into the room.

"You look like pictures from my high-school yearbook," Dad gasped.

"That's exactly the effect we wanted," Pippa said.

"But this isn't a costume party," Mom said. "It's a prom."

"Same thing." Pippa twirled around so the taffeta skirt ballooned out, and the room filled up with a moldy smell.

"What will your dates say?" Mom wondered.

The doorbell rang. We'd soon find out.

Not only was it "the dates," but the rest of the Lomax Thrift Shop window.

Nobody said a word, and then suddenly everybody began to talk at once.

"What do you call this?" Pippa demanded.

"A joke," Pete answered. "Like sending those invites and then pretending you didn't."

"We never sent you invitations to the prom," Anitra stormed. "You sent them to us."

"Oh, sure." Jojo rolled his eyes. "I suppose you didn't write those stupid notes. 'How I'd love to dance the night away in your arms,' " he quoted from *P.S. I've Got a Crush on You*.

"You thought I'd write that?" Anitra threw one of Mrs. Gilchrist's beaded bags at him and hit Pete.

"Was this your idea of a joke?" Pippa said.

"No, it was your idea of a trick," Pete answered.

"Stop!" I hollered.

"It was *our* idea for Project Romance. We wrote the notes and sent the roses."

"Project what?" Anitra and Pippa and Jojo and Pete all said at once. My mother and father just looked at us. I wondered what would happen next.

What happened next was the doorbell rang again.

It was Lucas and Charlie.

"What are you doing here?" I asked. For a moment, I completely forgot I had asked them to come by.

"Don't you remember?" Lucas whispered. "You told us we could stop by and see the guys we wrote those notes for."

"You don't have to whisper," I whispered. "They know about Project Romance."

"No, we don't." Pippa shook her head. "Maybe you better tell us."

"We wanted you and Anitra to start acting like the real teens in Sakrinhill Quints and Sugerwater High. Only our plans worked in reverse. You're fighting with your boyfriends, and you won't go to the prom."

"We aren't fighting now that we know the truth," Anitra said. "And I don't see why we shouldn't go to the prom."

"After all, we've got gowns and nails and eyelashes and shoes." Pippa twirled on her toes.

"And we all match," Jojo pointed out. "The Lomax Thrift Shop Look."

"So what are we waiting for?" Pete said. "It's prom time."

Anitra picked up Mrs. Gilchrist's beaded bag from the floor. Pippa adjusted Mrs. Wong's wig. Dad said, "Hold it," Mom said, "Heads together," and the camera went click, click.

They waved good-bye.
The door closed.

I felt as if I had finished the last of the paperback romances, and somehow even though it was all wrong it had turned out all right.

"I don't think I'm interested in romance anymore," Hermione said.

"Maybe we just didn't know how to do it," I said.

"How can you say that? We read Sakrinhill one through fifteen and Sugerwater one through twenty-five."

"But those are books. Maybe real life is different," I said.

"Excuse me," Lucas said, tapping my shoulder impatiently. "Let's go or we'll

miss out on the chips and punch, and I really want to dance with you, Rosy."

"You do?"

I looked at Lucas very hard. He didn't seem to be kidding. He wanted to take me to the dance. He wanted to dance with me. I remembered how he was always on my corner, playing catch, bird-watching a blue jay, dribbling a basketball. Was he really my secret admirer?

We said good-bye to my parents and went to buzz the elevator. This wasn't like Sakrinhill or Sugerwater or Anitra and Pippa. This wasn't like Project Romance.

I whispered in Hermione's ear, "You're right about something."

"What?" She looked surprised.

"Tell you later."

We all got into the elevator and I really had to laugh because it was happening right under my nose and I never knew it.

Rosy's Romance.